P9-DEZ-347

The
Christmas
Wish

The Christmas Wish

J. GRIBBIN HUTCHINSON

ATHENEUM BOOKS

Without the persistence, dedication, and enthusiasm of Barbara Markowitz, my agent, this book would be residing exclusively within my computer. Barbara Markowitz will always be Santa Claus to me.

I want to also thank my wonderful editors, Sarah Caguiat and Ana Cerro, for their insight; my wife and daughter for being my wife and daughter; Richard Mandel and Mitchell Salem for their friendship; and the six best brothers and sisters in the world.

Atheneum Books
An imprint of Simon & Schuster
1230 Avenue of the Americas
New York, New York 10020

Book design by Nina Barnett
The text of this book is set in Goudy.

First Edition
Printed in the United States of America
10 9 8 7 6 5 4 3 2

Library of Congress Cataloging-in-Publication Data
Hutchinson, J. Gribbin (John Gribbin)
The Christmas wish / J. Gribbin Hutchinson.—1st ed.
p. cm.
Summary: David's father, having died one Christmas morning,
continues to appear and visit with him at key moments in David's life.
ISBN 0-689-81158-6
[1. Fathers and sons—Fiction. 2. Ghosts—Fiction.
3. Death—Fiction. 4. Christmas—Fiction.] I. Title.
PZ7.H9617Ch 1997
[Fic]—dc21 96-50237

To the memory of my father

The
Christmas
Wish

Chapter One

My father died on Christmas morning when I was six years old. His heart stopped beating while he was putting together my first two-wheeler.

I had asked the phony Santa Claus at the department store for a bicycle, but he just patted my head and handed me a candy cane, without making any promises. I couldn't sleep too well that Christmas Eve, wondering if the department store Santa had told the real Santa about my bike.

Before the sun was up, I decided to tiptoe downstairs to sneak a peek under the tree. My parents had made me promise at least a hundred times not to open any presents without waking them first, but I knew that a bicycle would be much too large a present to wrap, and I wouldn't have to open a thing.

From the top of the stairs, I could see my mother sitting in the tiny rocking chair that had come from England. The antique chair in the hallway was supposed to be for decoration only because it was much too old and valuable to waste on sitting. My mother was dressed in the red robe my father had given her on their first Christmas together, almost three years before I was born. She was crying softly into the furry white collar of the robe. Every time she rocked, the little chair creaked and groaned with grief, but it did not break.

I came down four steps until I could just see inside the living room. Two strange men in white uniforms were pinching my father's nose and blowing air into his mouth. When my father didn't respond to their kisses, the men in white pressed down hard on his chest and shouted: "Come on, Mr.

Connors, come on! Don't give up on us." But my father wasn't listening. After another minute or two, the two men shook their heads sadly and told each other it was no use. My father was never coming back.

I saw the bicycle before my mother dragged me by my pajama sleeves into the kitchen. It was made of shiny green steel, just like the one I had asked for. The frame was attached, but not the seat, or handlebars, or wheels. When I saw my father on the floor, holding a screwdriver in his hand, I knew right away that Santa Claus wasn't real. My parents had bought my Christmas presents in a store, and they'd made up the whole Santa Claus story.

My mother left with the ambulance. She sat in the back beside my father. The men in white drove away slowly, without bothering to turn on the siren. Our next-door neighbor, Mr. Paul, stayed with me until my mother came back. Mr. Paul was much much older than my parents, and he lived alone without any wife or children of his own.

My mother said that Mr. Paul was always pleased

to keep me company because he was sad and lonely living all by himself. I never thought Mr. Paul seemed a bit sad. He had no hair, or eyebrows either, and his ears were big and loose and seemed barely attached to his head. His entire face was white like paste, not the ordinary color of skin. Mr. Paul smiled or laughed just about all the time, and he walked with a limp because he had been sick with polio when he was six years old. I thought his last name should have been his first name, and I didn't know then whether he had any first name at all. Mr. Paul wrote thick, heavy books about people who were famous and dead, like actors, presidents, comedians, and criminals. I wasn't old enough to read them.

Even though there was plenty of snow and ice outside, Mr. Paul came over wearing only a white nightshirt and green slippers. His slippers were badly torn in front, and I could see that he hadn't cut his toenails in a very long time. Mr. Paul's pink rabbit-like eyes were wet with tears, but he was trying awfully hard to smile, which made his face look even stranger than usual. When Mr. Paul held me tight and promised that everything would be okay, I squirmed out of his grip and ran to the living room, stopping right at the spot where my father had been.

"It's a handsome tree, David," Mr. Paul said. "A magnificent specimen."

I had gone to the YMCA with my father to pick out the tree that year. It was my first time, and he gave me the choice of anything in the lot that cost twenty dollars or less. My father must have twirled around at least fifty different trees so that I could examine their size and shape from every possible angle.

"You can't be too careful," he had warned me. "The tree might be full in front but too skimpy in back. Or a lopsided-looking tree might be perfect once you see the whole picture. Don't be fooled by first appearances."

After spending nearly an hour outside in the cold, I finally settled on a blue spruce. It was almost eight feet tall, and its branches were thick and full from top to bottom and all the way around. My father made me carry my end to the car, but it was much too heavy and awkward to lift, and I dragged it along the ground.

"Just a little further, David," he said, encouraging me. "That's Daddy's grown-up boy."

Christmas morning was just beginning to dawn outside, but the sun was hidden behind an ugly ceiling of cold, gray winter clouds. I concentrated only on the tree. It was bright and pretty, with blinking white lights, shiny tinsel, and glass ornaments that were older than I was, and some even older than my parents. I didn't think we had any ornaments quite as old as Mr. Paul.

I shook a handful of the branches and dozens of dead needles fell like dry, green snow on top of the unopened packages. I cut my thumb as I pulled my hand away from the sharp tree, and it started to bleed, one giant drop of red running slowly down my finger. My father had forgotten to show me how to test the needles to make sure they were fresh and moist, so that the tree would still be well by Christmas.

Except for my bicycle, all the presents were wrapped, and I wanted to rip open each and every one without stopping to look at what was inside. I couldn't think about anything except what a horrible Christmas this would be, now that both Santa Claus and my father were gone. Waiting for a fat old man to slide down our chimney in the middle of the night suddenly seemed like kid stuff to me. Santa Claus was a fake, my father was dead, and somehow I knew that Christmas was to blame for it all.

While I was staring at the tree, Mr. Paul finished putting together my bicycle, first the wheels, then the handlebars, and finally the seat. In less than ten minutes, the job was done.

"I don't know if I've ever seen a more impressive machine," Mr. Paul said to me, polishing the green steel with the sleeve of his nightshirt.

It was the very best kid's bike—a Stingray—and it could stand up to almost anything. The wheels were wide and thick, and it had three different gears for pedaling up and down hills. The seat was shaped like a large banana, big enough for two. I could see my reflection in the handlebars, they were so shiny and new. The steel was a dark shade of green, even darker than our tree. It was just the right color for a boy's bike.

"Perhaps you'd like to take her for a test run," Mr. Paul suggested.

I didn't answer him right away because I couldn't take my eyes off my new bike. I wanted to climb on that bike and ride and ride for hours and weeks until I was so far away no one would ever find me.

"It's all right, David," Mr. Paul assured me. "Round the block a few times might do you a world of good. You can throw on a coat over your pajamas."

Without saying a word to Mr. Paul, I walked the bike outside to the back porch. As Mr. Paul leaned over to help me carry the bike down to the yard, I let it drop. It tumbled down twelve cement steps and crashed onto the icy path below. My father had shoveled the snow off the walk just two days earlier, but with all the excitement about Christmas, he never got around to sprinkling salt on the walk to melt away the ice. When I reached the bottom of the steps, I was surprised to see that the bike wasn't even damaged. Nothing had fallen off, and it still looked brand new.

I started to jump up and down on the sturdy green steel. Finally the metal began to bend and the shine turned to scratches. Mr. Paul watched from the top of the porch steps, but he didn't try to stop me. With a great burst of strength, I threw the broken bike into the middle of the yard, where it landed in a deep pile of snow. I didn't ride the Stingray that day or any other day. Later that morning, when I went out to salt the walk, the bicycle was gone. I never asked anyone what had happened to it.

When spring came, and the weather started turning warm again, I found the kickstand to the Stingray in my father's workroom. He must have forgotten all about it. I decided to keep the kickstand—for my next bike.

Chapter Two

By the time I turned eight years old, I was tall, skinny, and nearsighted. Six months after my father's death, we had moved across town to an apartment in a two-family house. My mother said we didn't need a big place all to ourselves, but I knew that she didn't have enough money to keep our old home.

Mr. Henderson and his daughter lived on the left side of the house. Jennifer Henderson and I were in the same class at school. She was tall, skinny, and nearsighted, just like me, but pretty enough to make a boy my age start talking to girls. Jennifer ran faster than I did, and she could hit a baseball farther, and punch harder, too. She also happened to be the smartest person in the entire third grade, and late at night, when she was supposed to be asleep, I could hear Jennifer through the open window to her bedroom practicing her state capitals. Pretty soon, I knew my capitals, too, just from listening to her.

But Jennifer wasn't the best at everything, which made me like her even more. Our music teacher made Jennifer hum along to the songs at school assemblies because she couldn't sing on key. I could draw much better than she could, especially animals, and her penmanship was awful. She almost always lost to me in checkers, and I won in Ping-Pong close to half the time. Those were the games I always suggested we play.

Mrs. Henderson lived far away, somewhere in Europe, I think. I didn't know anything about her, except that the Hendersons were divorced, and my mother said that Mrs. Henderson needed time alone to solve her problems. Jennifer wasn't allowed to see her mother, or to write her letters, but she kept an old black-and-white photograph of Mrs. Henderson on her dresser, in a blue frame with pink flowers shaped like tears along the edges.

After my father died, my mother became a real-estate agent to support the two of us. She sold and rented homes to strangers six, sometimes seven, days a week, and when she wasn't working, she was usually too exhausted to play with me. I learned to make hamburgers, tuna-fish sandwiches, and chicken potpies, and, after a while, I did the cooking almost every night. After dinner, my mother paid bills or read the newspaper in the darkest corner of the living room, cuddled up like a puppy on my father's favorite chair. Most nights she would fall asleep in the soft, green leather chair, and I would cover her with a flannel blanket so she wouldn't catch a cold.

Mr. Paul came to visit us often, at least once a week. He had never learned to drive, so he came in a taxi. Sometimes, Mr. Paul would meet me after school and take me by taxi into New York City. We watched the Wall Street traders buy and sell stocks, we rode elevators to the tops of all the tallest buildings, and we ate at fancy restaurants that served strange food in funny-shaped shells with names I almost always mispronounced.

Our favorite place to visit together was the Metropolitan Museum of Art. Sometimes, Mr. Paul and I would spend an entire afternoon studying just one painting. Mr. Paul taught me everything he knew about colors and angles and shapes, as well as what he called the "artists' intentions." But when I asked Mr. Paul if he could teach me how to paint, he shook his head.

"I can enjoy the pictures with you, David," Mr. Paul explained, "but when it comes to the nuts and bolts of how to do it, I'm afraid I'm no use to you. Why, I can't even paint my own living room walls."

I wouldn't let Mr. Paul take me to see the *Nutcracker*, the Macy's Thanksgiving Day Parade, the tree at Rockefeller Center, or anything that reminded me of Christmas, my least favorite day.

My mother said it was important for the two of

us to keep celebrating Christmas. The year after my father's death, she bought a small artificial tree for the hall table in the apartment, but we never got around to trimming it. We gave each other presents, but only things that were useful, like clothes, and kitchen utensils, and school supplies—nothing for fun. We didn't wrap any of the packages, and we told each other in advance exactly what we were going to buy, so there wouldn't be any more surprises on Christmas morning. With no Santa Claus to bother me, I slept like a baby on Christmas Eve.

My birthday, however, was a different situation completely. It was the one day of the year, the sixteenth of June, that belonged all to me, and no one—not my father, and certainly not Santa Claus—was going to spoil my fun.

A taxicab honked its horn outside our apartment just as my mother was smoothing the strawberry icing on her famous three-layer, homemade chocolate-chip cake. I ran out to help Mr. Paul, who was struggling with an enormous square box wrapped in silver, with a red satin bow spilling out over the sides.

"For the young Picasso, on the occasion of the eighth anniversary of his birth," Mr. Paul said to me as he presented his gift.

Inside the box were paints—oil paints, in multicolored toothpaste tubes, brushes in every size and shape, an easel, and hundreds of sheets of thick white paper.

"A painter's magic tools!" Mr. Paul exclaimed. "Take the blank canvas, David, and let your imagination run wild."

My mother smiled and handed me her gift. It was a round, gray hat made of rough cloth, with nothing in the front that flipped up or down.

"It's a beret," she said.

"What's a beret?" I asked.

"The official hat of every great painter in Paris," Mr. Paul said with a smile.

Suddenly I realized that I had an awful lot to learn about becoming an artist. "What if I can't teach myself to do it?" I asked, frightened by the enormous challenge I had in front of me.

"Oh, you're an artist all right." Mr. Paul nodded,

his pink little eyes blinking and twitching like a pinball machine. "That's the ticket for this particular young man."

"Your father was an artist," my mother said. "An illustrator."

I didn't know what an illustrator did exactly, but I did remember my father warning me not to play with any of the pictures in the square, thin black briefcase he carried back and forth to work.

I had tried not to think about my father since his death, but sometimes I could think of little else. I wanted very badly to understand why he had left us so suddenly, without even bothering to stop and say good-bye. As time passed, I was finding it harder and harder to remember little things about him, like the sound of his voice when he was especially angry or glad, or the exact color of his eyes. I was even finding it harder to remember the incredible joy I would feel deep down in my heart whenever he mussed all my hair. If my mother hadn't kept so many old photographs of my father all around the house, I think I might have forgotten him completely.

But right now, something other than my father was on my mind. After my birthday dinner was finished, I sat down directly across from my mother and Mr. Paul at the table and cleared my throat to get their attention. "I've been thinking," I said, blinking and twitching just like Mr. Paul. "I don't have a father. Mom doesn't have a husband. And you, Mr. Paul, don't have a wife. Why can't Mr. Paul be my father? You two could be husband and wife, and I could be Mr. Paul's son. We could be like a normal family. It's a pretty good idea, don't you think?"

Judging from the startled expressions on their faces, I could tell that my mother and Mr. Paul didn't think my idea was good at all. My mother tapped her fingers nervously on the table, while Mr. Paul rubbed his head in the spot where his eyebrows were supposed to be.

"It's not because of the presents and other stuff," I assured Mr. Paul. "If you said yes, you wouldn't have to buy me any more presents. You could even give the paints to someone else, to another boy who didn't have a father and really needed them."

Mr. Paul and my mother stared at each other, but they wouldn't look at me. They seemed to be trying to decide which one of them would speak first. Finally, Mr. Paul reached his long bony hand across the table and gently held my hand.

"Why, that's an ingenious idea, David," he said. "I certainly would be unhappy without the two of you around to take such good care of me."

"So, it's a deal?" I asked hopefully, even though I had a feeling I knew what he was going to say next.

"*But* marrying your mother won't make me your father," Mr. Paul explained. "You only get one father, David, one real father, and your father was a remarkable fellow. A most congenial man. It was a dreadful thing to have him taken away from you at such an early age, but he's watching over you, keeping his eyes on your progress. It's what your father gave you that helps make you who you are. Believe me, he's still alive inside you. Don't be afraid to ask for his help anytime you need it."

My mother nodded quietly in agreement.

I had no idea what Mr. Paul was talking about. If

I could have only one real father, I wanted someone else, a person I could see and feel and talk to. I was too grown-up now for fairy tales about Santa Claus, or dead people watching over me. I loved Mr. Paul, and he was here, where I could reach out and touch him. Mr. Paul liked me, I knew he did. He liked my mother, and my mother liked him. I didn't mind one bit that he was really old and fragile, like an antique. When Mr. Paul went home after visiting the two of us, he always came back. That's all that mattered.

I kept trying to persuade Mr. Paul and my mother to go along with my plan, but it was no use. They just weren't young enough to understand.

Three days later, I was alone in my bedroom, trying to paint a sailboat out at sea, and having a terrible time of it. I could make a pencil do almost anything because the tip was sharp and easy to control. But a paintbrush was soft and squishy, and the shape of the boat was all wrong. Choosing colors was even worse. I wanted the ocean to be blue, but not the dark, dangerous shade of blue that came in the tube Mr. Paul had given me. I needed to mix that blue with something lighter, but I didn't know which colors were right or how much of each to use.

After several hours of pure frustration, I quit trying, determined to give up painting for good. I tore the unfinished picture in two and threw it into the wastebasket. Then I changed into my pajamas, brushed my teeth, and went to bed.

When I woke up from a dream in the middle of the night, the lights were on, and my painting was resting on the easel. The paper wasn't torn or even crumpled. A man in a checkered, red flannel shirt and old, green, corduroy pants was sitting on my bed, mixing paints and whistling a tune I had heard many times before. When I sat up in bed, he turned around to face me. Almost instantly, I recognized my father.

He looked a little different, not quite the way I remembered him. My father had always been chubby, mostly in his stomach. But he'd gained a little more weight since his death—not a whole lot, maybe nine or ten pounds. His hair had once been dark black, just like mine, but it was colored now with streaks of silver, and he had grown a mustache, which was also mostly gray. For the past year and a half my father had continued to age, just as if he had been living all along.

I couldn't move for the first minute or two, terrified by the thought of being face-to-face with a real live ghost. But soon I started to relax. Except for the fact that he was dead, my father acted perfectly normal. His face was one giant smile, and my heart pounded with joy when he mussed all my hair.

"My, how you've changed, David," he said proudly. His voice was deep and sweet, like a musical instrument.

"You . . . you've changed, too," I stuttered.

"I suppose I have at that," he replied curiously, as though he hadn't thought about it before.

"Are you staying?" I asked.

"No, I'm afraid not."

"How did you get here?"

"I really can't say," he replied. "I'm not quite sure how it works."

"Are you still dead?"

"Well, I guess I'd have to answer yes to that. But then again, here I am, and there you are. We might as well make the best of it."

"But you can't stay," I reminded him.

"No," he agreed, "that's the part of it that can't be the same."

A hundred more questions raced inside my head, but I just looked into my father's gentle blue eyes and said nothing. He told me that our time together was limited, and we ought to get right down to business.

My father handed me a pencil and kept one for himself. Then he took the white canvas paper and began to sketch out very faintly the shape of a sailboat with the ocean underneath, the sky above, and the setting sun in the distance. When he was through, he grabbed the blue paint, and the white, and the green, and a few drops of water, and began to mix together a little bit from each tube on a flat tray, using more blue than all the other colors combined. He painted where he had sketched the sea, and slowly, waves started to toss the little sailboat.

But because the water was colored a light and peaceful shade of blue, like my father's eyes, I knew the boat was in no danger.

My father mixed red and yellow and orange paints for the sunset, and blue and white with just a touch of gray for the sky. He worked until the entire painting was finished except for the boat and its mast gusting in the wind.

"The rest is for you, David," he said to me. "Do you think you can manage it?"

I knew I could, and I nodded yes.

"Remember," my father said. "Use your pencil to trace. And don't forget, any color you want is in there. You just have to know how to find it."

My father winked at me, like we were sharing a secret. "Don't be afraid to let yourself dream a little."

Then he tucked me into bed and waited until I was tired enough to fall asleep.

"I'm sorry for going away, David," he said. "It couldn't be helped."

"It's okay," I assured him. "I understand." I really didn't understand a thing, but I didn't want my father to feel guilty about leaving us alone, just in case it hadn't been his fault.

My father laughed a big hearty laugh and started to climb out my bedroom window, which was on the third floor of the two-family house. I didn't think it the least bit strange that he didn't use the door.

Just as my father was ducking his head behind the curtains, I called out to him, "Will you be back?"

He looked confused and troubled as he pondered my question. "I really couldn't say," he answered. "I certainly hope so."

"I don't see why not," I added confidently.

He smiled again brightly. "Yes, I don't see why not," he repeated. "Of course, I can't speak for you, David, but it's my opinion that we've still got plenty left to talk about."

"Maybe when you come the next time, you could stay a little while longer," I suggested.

"I'll see if it can be arranged," my father replied, pleased to have received the invitation. "Pleasant dreams, David."

"Pleasant dreams," I answered him.

In an instant, my father was gone. Somewhere between the window and the yard below, he vanished out of sight. My father never said to keep our visit a secret, but I decided not to tell a single person what had taken place that night.

Chapter Three

It was a rainy Saturday morning in July, and I had four hours left to stop my mother from making the biggest mistake of her life.

She was about to marry Mr. Eddie Kravitz, who owned the new shoe store in town. My mother had met Mr. Kravitz just ten months earlier, when I needed a new pair of shoes for the first day of school. If I hadn't been growing two full sizes every three months, none of this would have happened.

The wedding had been carefully planned. As the

best man, I was supposed to hold the rings and stand right beside Mr. Kravitz. Mr. Paul would escort my mother down the aisle and "give her away," whatever that was supposed to mean. After the ceremony, Mr. Kravitz was going to throw a big party underneath a green-and-white circus tent that had been set up in his backyard. Then I would live with Mr. Paul for two weeks while Mr. Kravitz and my mother spent their honeymoon in Bermuda. During that time, the moving company would take all of our things from the two-family house we shared with the Hendersons to Mr. Kravitz's home twelve miles away. I would attend a new school, and Jennifer Henderson and I would probably never see each other again. My mother would be called Elizabeth Kravitz, but my last name would still be Connors.

It was your basic nightmare.

But that wasn't even the worst part. Everyone was forgetting about my father, even though he had been dead for less than three years. And, in a manner of speaking, he wasn't dead at all. My father had visited me only the one time, but I was sure he would return. Under the circumstances, my mother couldn't marry Mr. Kravitz, or any other man. Even if he could never move back home to live with us, my father would certainly be dropping by for visits now and again.

I really didn't have anything against Mr. Kravitz. He wasn't particularly clever, or funny, or handsome. In many ways, he was pretty strange, sort of an oddball, I guess you could say. But he did try awfully hard to be friendly and kind to my mother and me, and, in spite of myself, I couldn't quite manage to dislike him.

Mr. Kravitz was ten years older than my mother, but still much younger than Mr. Paul. He had long, curly black hair on the sides and in back, but the rest of his head was bald, and he combed his hair across the front to try and make you think he wasn't bald at all. He was skinny like Mr. Paul and short like my father. He always wore a fresh white carnation on the lapel of his jacket, and he would bring my mother a dozen white carnations each time he called on her. He owned a red foreign sports car with a convertible top, but he always drove ten miles below the speed limit and stopped at yellow lights.

When he was younger, Mr. Kravitz had been an actor and had played small parts in several Broadway musicals. When you least expected it, he would start singing old show tunes in his soft, pretty voice, and invite everyone within earshot to please join in. He laughed and cried loudly when we watched television, even if the program wasn't especially funny or sad. He danced with my mother without any music playing, and had a strange habit of kissing me on both cheeks whenever I greeted him at the door. He called my mother his "salvation" and me "Davey Boy." My mother called Mr. Kravitz her "gallant knight," and I could tell she loved him very much.

I had hoped that my mother and Mr. Kravitz would just remain friends so I would never have to share my secret. But I had to do something to stop this wedding, whatever it took, and time was running out.

Convincing my mother that my father had gained weight and grown a mustache *after* his death was not going to be easy. When Mr. Paul had said that my father was keeping his eyes on my progress, I don't think a private painting lesson in my bedroom was quite what he'd had in mind.

I found my mother sitting in the kitchen, surrounded by dozens of boxes all packed for the move. She was wearing the old, red robe my father had given her and a new pair of glittery, silver slippers from Mr. Kravitz's store. Her hair was up in curlers and she was humming the same tune my father had been whistling the night he taught me how to paint.

"Do you have enough money to last you while we're gone?" she asked.

"Yes," I answered her.

"Did Mr. Paul give you the keys to his house?"

"Yes," I said again.

"Do your shoes need to be shined?"

"No," I lied.

"Do you have film for the camera?"

"Yes."

"Well, we're almost ready then," my mother said, breathing a deep sigh of relief. "Nothing to do now but wait."

My mother was a pretty woman, even in a bathrobe and curlers. Her long brown hair was straight and thick, her skin dark and soft. When she smiled, you could see all her teeth, even the ones in back. If she was especially happy and excited, like today, she smiled all the time.

When my father was alive, my mother used to play the piano and sing to us, funny songs mostly, about dragons and pirates and mermaids. I couldn't remember any of the words. On "Special Supper Nights," the three of us would dress up for dinner in our most elegant, dress-up clothes. I would wear a navy blue suit with short pants that I never really liked. My mother would put on a long, green silk gown that had belonged to her mother and wrap her hair in circles high on top of her head. And my father would dress in a black tuxedo that he'd bought at a second-hand store. On his head, he wore a magician's top hat.

Once we were seated my mother would turn out the lights and we would eat by the light of a hundred gold candles, glittering like tiny stars all around our dining room. After the meal my father would pull out a bouquet of red and blue plastic flowers from inside his magic hat.

"For you," he'd say to my mother as he presented her with the flowers. "For-ever."

When I was old enough, my father promised to pull a white rabbit out of his top hat, especially for me.

The three of us must have done at least a million other silly things when we were still a family, but unfortunately, funny songs at the piano and Special Supper Nights were all I could remember.

"I like Mr. Kravitz," I said to my mother.

"He likes you," she told me. "You really should try to call him Eddie."

"He's too old to call by his first name," I said.

"Suit yourself," she replied.

"Do you remember when I wanted you to marry Mr. Paul?" I asked.

"Yes," my mother answered with a smile, showing all her teeth. "That was sweet."

"Do you remember what he said?"

"Not exactly," my mother answered softly, but I had the feeling that she remembered every word.

"He said no one could take Daddy's place," I reminded her. "He said a person only gets one father, one real father, and you agreed with him."

My mother stood up and started washing dishes that had been washed the night before. "Mr. Paul was right," she said to me. "Eddie can't replace your father. But he can love you *like* a father, if you let him."

When I didn't respond, my mother turned off the water and dried her hands on the red robe. I noticed for the first time that almost all of the buttons on the old robe were missing, and the white furry collar was now a dirty shade of gray.

"You miss your father an awful lot, don't you, David?" she asked.

"I miss him when he's not here," I answered her.

My mother seemed puzzled by my remark but she let it pass without a word.

"I miss him, too, David," she said.

"Maybe it's not such a good idea for you to get married then," I suggested. "I'm sure Mr. Kravitz would understand. He's very understanding."

"David, your father's gone," my mother said. "We have to try and do our best without him. He would have wanted it that way."

"I'm not so sure," I replied.

"We'll always have his memory," my mother assured me.

"What if I told you that Daddy's still with us?" I asked.

"Of course he is," she agreed. "That's a lovely thought."

"You don't understand," I protested. "He's *really* with us." As I took a deep breath and prepared to tell my mother everything, I noticed that my father was sitting at the opposite end of the table.

He was wearing a plain blue cotton robe and was eating an apple. He had grown a beard to go along with his mustache, and his long messy hair was now almost completely gray.

"David, I'd like to have a word with you," my father said. "In private."

I was much too excited to do what he asked. I don't know where or how he had gotten his information, but my father had arrived just in time to stop the wedding.

"Am I ever glad to see you," I said out loud.

"David, is something wrong?" my mother asked.

"I'm afraid you're on your own with this one," my father said.

I saw my mother looking frantically around the room for a third person, and I realized that she could see no one but me or hear anything but the sound of my voice.

"You're invisible?" I asked my father, still talking out loud.

"Not to you," he answered, with a mischievous twinkle in his eye.

"That's swell," I replied sarcastically. "Terrific."

Now that I was conducting a full-blown conversation with thin air, my mother rushed around the table to feel my forehead.

"David, David, snap out of it," she pleaded. "I'm sorry. I had no idea. We'll call off the wedding."

I wanted to shout for joy that my mother was changing her plans, but much to my surprise, my father seemed in no mood to celebrate. He rose from his chair. Soon, the three of us were huddled together, like we were posing for a picture. My father spoke into my left ear, my mother into my right.

"Tell her that you're feeling perfectly fine," my father ordered me. "Go on, David. Do as I say."

"I'm feeling perfectly fine," I assured my mother, obeying my father's commands.

My mother wasn't convinced. I turned to my father for more instructions.

"It must be something you ate," my father said.

"I wish," I mumbled back at him.

My father was not amused.

"It must be something I ate," I told my mother.

"Tell your mother that you just wanted her to know you would never forget me," my father said. "I'm always on your mind."

"I just wanted you to know I would never forget

me," I said. "I mean, him—I would never forget Daddy."

"Your father's an awfully hard person to forget," my mother said.

"You're telling me," I agreed.

Before I could catch my breath, my father began barking out more commands.

"Now tell your mother that you're very happy for her and Eddie, and you want them to be married today."

I frowned and didn't say a word.

"David, that's an order," he said sternly.

I still refused to obey. "I won't do it," I whispered back at him.

My mother heard me and started worrying all over again. "You look pale," she told me. "Why don't you rest."

"David, I'm still your father," my father reminded me. "You only get one father. One real father. Remember? Like it or not, you're stuck with me."

"I'm very happy for you and Mr. Kravitz," I said.

"Eddie," my father interrupted me. "Call him Eddie, like your mother asked you to do."

"I'm very happy for you and Eddie," I corrected myself. "I want you to be married today."

"David, are you sure?" my mother asked.

"Yes, you're sure," my father said.

"Yes, I'm sure," I repeated, though I wasn't sure at all.

"I want you to be okay with all of this, David," my mother told me. "It's a big step for both of us."

"You're okay," my father said. "Eddie's a great guy."

"I'm okay," I said. "Eddie's okay."

"Now give your mother a kiss," my father said. "And meet me upstairs."

I kissed my mother, then followed the sound of my father's footsteps marching up the stairs. Now that he was a ghost, my father was a lot more bossy than he'd ever been when he was alive.

When I got to the top floor of the apartment, my father was changing into the old, second-hand tuxedo he used to wear on Special Supper Nights. It had been packed away since his death, but he knew exactly where to find it. All of the buttons were missing from the jacket, and the whole tuxedo smelled like mothballs and dust. My father had put on another ten pounds since our last visit, and as hard as he tried, he couldn't fasten the waistband on his slacks. When he started struggling with the top button of his shirt, his cheeks turned all red and tight and puffy, like a balloon about to burst. Suddenly, he erupted into laughter, releasing a hurricane of air. It was a deep, throaty, jolly laugh, deeper than it used to be.

"Looks like I've been eating a few too many sweets," he confessed.

"What's going on here?" I demanded to know.

"I've missed you, David," my father said, ignoring my question.

"What are you doing?" I asked, determined to get some answers.

"Dressing for a wedding," he replied matter-of-factly. "In my most elegant dress-up clothes."

"You're going to Mom's wedding?" I asked.

"You wanted me to visit a little while longer this time," he answered. "I've cleared the whole day."

"You're not actually planning to wear that old thing?" I asked, referring to his smelly tuxedo.

"And why not?" he asked. "I'm not going to have my nine-year-old son looking nicer than his father."

"It doesn't fit you anymore, that's why," I told him. "You're too fat."

My father pulled the zipper on his pants up as far as it would go and somehow managed to button the top of his shirt.

"Nonsense," he objected, his feelings obviously hurt. "It fits perfectly. Better than new, in fact."

My father sat down on a cardboard box to tie his dirty shoes, but the box collapsed, tossing him to the floor. In the crash, the top button popped off his shirt and flew like a tiny Frisbee halfway across the room.

"Well, maybe not perfectly," he admitted.

"You never told me no one else could see you," I said.

"Did I neglect to mention that little detail?" my father asked guiltily, knowing full well that he had.

"It's like having a talking horse," I complained.

"Don't call your father a talking horse," he scolded me. "You're developing an awfully fresh mouth for such a little boy. It's not the least bit attractive."

"I'm not a little boy anymore," I protested. "Thanks to you."

"No, I guess you're not," my father said sadly. "You've grown up much too quickly to suit me. . . . How have you been, David?"

"Lousy," I said. "My father's invisible and my mother's about to marry someone else. It's not exactly a dream come true."

"That's why I'm here," my father responded happily.

"Are you going to stop her?" I asked, my high-pitched voice cracking with hope.

"I'm going to stop you from stopping her," he replied. "Now that you're such a big boy, we need to clear up a few important details."

My father took my hand and walked me to the rear of the storage area, where there were two large armchairs wrapped in filthy white sheets. He removed a small brown pipe from the jacket pocket of his tuxedo. Without lighting the pipe or filling it with tobacco, he blew large rings of white smoke that floated like soft summer clouds above us before vanishing into air.

Once he was comfortable, my father began to ask me questions, one right after another, until my head was spinning.

"You love your mother, don't you, David?"

"Yes," I answered him.

"And you want her to be happy?"

"Of course," I said.

"And this Mr. Kravitz fellow, he's not too bad, is he?"

"Not *too* bad," I confessed. "Considering . . ."

"Now what kind of a husband do you think I could be to your mother, in my present . . . *unusual* condition?" he asked.

"Not especially good?" I replied, hoping my father would disagree.

"Exactly," he said.

"I'm confused," I told my father. "If I can have only one father, why can Mom have two husbands?"

"Someday you're going to move away and start a family of your own," my father explained. "You and I can't have your mother spending the rest of her days alone just because I'm dead. That sounds a little selfish to me, don't you think?"

"If you say so," I replied, not at all persuaded.

"We both know that your mother hasn't been very happy these past few years," my father said. "Do you think she's happy now?"

"Maybe," I said, not wanting to surrender too much.

"Tell me the truth," he insisted.

"You know very well that she is," I admitted. "But you're not really dead."

"The two of us have a *special* arrangement," my father explained. "Since we didn't have much of a chance to get to know each other the first time around, we've been given a little extra time."

"How long?" I asked him.

My father scratched his dirty beard from top to bottom, carefully considering my question.

"Well, I suppose that depends on you," he replied.

Suddenly, I thought I understood how this special arrangement worked.

"Someday, you'll be invisible to me, too, like all the others," I said. "That's right, isn't it?"

"Not until you're ready."

"Will you tell me when?" I asked him.

"No, *you'll* tell me," my father answered.

I couldn't understand how I would be able to tell my dead father when he was going to become invisible to me.

We sat together in silence for another minute or two. Then I walked over to my father's chair, sat on his lap, and wrapped my arms around his neck. I wasn't little anymore, and I was afraid that I would be too heavy for him, but my father didn't seem to mind.

"Is it really right for Mom to get married again?" I asked him, staring straight into his truthful eyes.

"I wouldn't be here if you didn't think so," my father replied.

"Are you sure you won't be too upset to see her with someone else?" I asked.

"David, I want your mother to remember the time we had together with great happiness," my father explained. "If she doesn't spend the rest of her life alone, I know she always will."

After I had exhausted all of my objections, my father led me to my bedroom and helped me dress for the wedding.

He tried to teach me how to tie a bow tie, explaining that it was no different from tying a shoelace. But when he finished his lesson, both of our ties looked absolutely awful, like two giant black spiders drooping down our collars. Come to think of it, on Special Supper Nights, my father's tie had always been loose and lopsided, nothing like a shoelace.

My father combed some blue, gooey jelly through my hair to keep it in place. He splashed my cheeks with some men's after-shave, even though my first shave was still a few years off. I clipped red suspenders to my father's unbuckled pants so they wouldn't fall down during the ceremony. We spat on each other's shoes and polished the pointy black tips with the sleeves of our jackets. After we were dressed, we admired ourselves in the full-length mirror, stopping to add some final touches.

Something was missing. I raced back upstairs to the attic, returning with the magician's top hat. The edges were torn and ragged, but the soft black silk still sparkled in the light. My father was fat all over now, and the top hat tilted to the right, nearly spilling off his head.

"A perfect fit," he said cheerfully.

"Perfect," I lied. "You look elegant."

"Yes, David," he said. "I do believe we do."

My father and I were an odd pair. To look at us, no one would have ever guessed we were related. I was tall and lanky and shaped like a golf club. He was short and round and furry, like a giant tennis ball.

When my father and I walked downstairs, my

mother made a big fuss about my suit. She insisted that I pose for a picture.

"You're the best-looking best man I've ever seen," she said.

"I'll second that sentiment," my father said.

"Just the youngest," I corrected my parents. "It's not the same thing."

When I refused to smile, my father snapped open his top hat and pulled out a bouquet of plastic flowers. I started laughing and my mother took the picture.

"Your turn," I said to my mother, grabbing the camera away from her.

"David, I'm not even dressed," she protested.

When my mother wasn't looking, I signaled to my father to join her in the picture.

"It won't work, David," my father warned me.

"I know," I said to both my parents. "But please do it anyway—just this once."

"If you insist," my mother said, who had no idea my father was standing right beside her, probably for the very last time.

"You're the boss," my father said, as he put his arm around my mother's shoulder.

I took the plastic flowers and handed them to my mother. She looked puzzled, no doubt wondering what magic I'd used to make them appear. But she recognized them immediately.

"For you," I said to her.

"For-ever," she replied.

Then I looked through the viewer and pressed the shutter, staring at a picture too magnificent for any camera to find.

My father sat in the back of the tent where no one could see him, though no one would have seen him wherever he sat. His eyesight had gotten worse since his death, and he wore a pair of small, wire-framed glasses throughout the ceremony.

As Mr. Paul escorted my mother down the aisle, Eddie began to cry, and I offered him my handkerchief to dry his eyes. "It's a glorious day," he whispered to me, as he fixed my messy tie. Eddie made a perfect bow in a matter of seconds.

"Yes, Eddie," I agreed. "Glorious."

I felt just the least bit sad when my mother and Eddie were pronounced man and wife, but I bit my lip, smiled a big, broad smile, and wished them all the best.

My father ate four slices of chocolate wedding cake during the reception in Eddie's backyard. He watched from the porch while I danced with my mother and toasted her happiness. When I came back to the porch with a fifth slice of cake, my father was gone.

On the long rectangular table piled high with wedding presents, my father had left behind a special gift, just for me. I waved my hands over the magician's top hat and pulled out an enormous white rabbit.

Chapter Four

My little brother was born less than a year after the wedding. Eddie and my mother called him their "little miracle."

We were first introduced to each other at the hospital, during one of his endless afternoon naps. His name was Samuel Edward Kravitz—Samuel after Eddie's uncle Samuel from Coney Island, New York, Edward after Eddie. Kravitz was, of course, the last name of everyone in my new family, everyone, that is, but me.

My brother was soft and wet and pink; his skin was like an old wrinkled sponge. He had a full head of oily black hair, but he was missing all his teeth. When I tried to hold Samuel, he protested so loudly that his entire body started turning blue, and he never once opened his eyes to greet me. He even spat in my face when I bent down to kiss his flabby cheeks, just so I would know how dangerous he could be.

Eddie and my mother thought that Samuel was the cutest, cleverest, most adorable child they had ever seen, but in my view, babies all looked and acted pretty much the same. Samuel was no exception.

Once my mother and Eddie found out a child was on the way, life in our house quickly began to change. I moved out of my bedroom, so that the baby's nursery would be closer to Eddie and my mother's room. I painted my old room blue, sprinkling the ceiling with splashes of white and orange and red to resemble the sky and the sun. With the help of two instruction manuals, Eddie and I spent four full months building a baby's crib. Neither one of us had ever used a saw or a drill before, and after the job was finished, we had to stick a book of Mother Goose rhymes under the shortest leg to keep the crib from tilting.

After Samuel came home to live with us, nothing was the same. First, there was the matter of sleep—no one was getting enough of it. My new brother did most of his sleeping in the daytime, when Eddie was at work and I was at school. At nighttime, Samuel preferred to cry, the louder the better, for hours at a time. Just as soon as all the lights were out and my head hit the pillow, Samuel would wake up, which meant he was hungry, or wet, or ready to be entertained.

Next, there were the chores. Keeping a newborn baby happy meant an awful lot of work. My mother still sold real estate, and she wasn't always home in the evenings. Eddie and I took turns changing Samuel's diaper, heating Samuel's bottle, and bathing Samuel in the sink. When my mother *was* home, she was busy with the baby, which meant that

Eddie and I cooked the meals, cleaned the house, and watched TV all by ourselves.

Last, but not least, there was the fuss. No one talked about anything but that little nuisance in my old bedroom. Samuel this. Samuel that. Just wiggling his tiny fingers and toes was worth an entire roll of film. Eddie and my mother asked me to paint pictures of some of my brother's most memorable moments. Samuel eating. Samuel spitting up. Samuel crying, which wasn't memorable at all. If Samuel so much as opened his eyes and gurgled at the same time, they thought he was a genius.

With all of my added responsibilities, I felt more like a grown-up than a ten year old. Together, Eddie, my mother, and I were raising Samuel, but every once in a while I couldn't help but wonder who was raising me.

After my father died I had to grow up in a hurry, and there wasn't much time to spare for silly fun and games. But when my mother married Eddie, everything changed for a while, and I felt I was catching up on some of the laughter I had missed.

Almost instantly, the three of us became a family, as though we had been together all along. We went camping in the woods, and my mother taught "her two helpless men" how to pitch a tent. We tried skiing, but Eddie and I spent most of the day rolling sideways down the hill.

My mother started playing the piano again, and I memorized the words to all of Eddie's favorite songs. We watched old movies together and acted out the parts. Whenever we ate in a restaurant, Eddie and I wore fresh white carnations on our jackets, and we both escorted my mother to her chair, each holding one of her arms. With my mother as my partner, Eddie showed me how to dance the waltz, the foxtrot, the alley cat, and the twist. Together, Eddie and I learned to change a tire, plant flowers in the garden, fix a leaky faucet, and replace a worn-out fuse. For those first five months, the three of us were having so much fun I didn't have any time for painting or to think about the past. But now that Samuel was the star of every picture, I felt there wasn't room for me, and I was thinking all the time.

It wasn't all the attention Samuel was getting that really made me fume. My parents must have thought I was the cutest baby ever born, too, so I figured that Samuel probably deserved his chance to be the cutest now. The problem was different, something I didn't know quite how to explain, and not Samuel's fault at all.

Before I knew it, my brother was almost six months old and starting to crawl. Since neither one of us was moving out any time soon, I was learning to tolerate him, but my progress was slow. If I made an especially ridiculous face or tried to drink his bottle, Samuel would start laughing, or wiggling his tiny fingers. Sometimes, when no one was watching, I would drop to the floor on my hands and knees and give Samuel a pony ride around the nursery.

One afternoon in February, my mother was out selling real estate, Eddie was busy shoveling snow, and I was minding Samuel. After a ten-minute pony ride and two extra bottles of milk, I finally convinced my brother to take his afternoon nap. When

I went downstairs to get some popcorn and watch TV, I found the refrigerator door wide open and the kitchen a mess. My father was at the table, making himself a snack.

"Do you have any baloney, please?" he asked politely.

"I don't think so," I answered. "How about ham?"

"Ham will do nicely," he said. "With a little cheese, swiss cheese, if you have it. And lettuce, of course. Don't forget the tomatoes," he reminded me. "Very thinly sliced."

"How about mustard?" I asked.

"Yes, mustard's a must," he said. "I don't suppose you have any pepperoni? I'm very partial to pepperoni these days."

"I'm sure we do," I replied. "Eddie loves pepperoni."

"I'd prefer a large roll to bread," my father said. "No seeds. I'm allergic to seeds."

"I'll look," I said. "I don't remember seeing any rolls."

"Oh, we must have some rolls," my father remarked confidently. "You might also keep your eyes peeled for a dill pickle," he continued. "Two dill pickles, in fact. And a large glass of milk. If it's not too much trouble."

I was surprised to find a fresh bag of seedless rolls in the back of the breadbasket and exactly two dill pickles hiding out in the bottom of a jar in the refrigerator. My father supervised my work while I fixed his sandwich, making absolutely certain that I applied the correct amount of each ingredient. But before I was even finished slicing the tomatoes, my father's thoughts turned to dessert. He helped himself to three pieces of apple pie and a fistful of freshly baked chocolate-chip cookies.

Given my father's mighty appetite, I wasn't surprised to see that he had gained more weight. His beard had grown another two inches and was badly in need of a trim. He had continued to age, but not very much, just about what you might expect for the amount of time he'd been away.

The temperature outside was close to freezing,

but my father was dressed in a short-sleeved white sports shirt and red tennis shorts. On his feet he wore a pair of black-and-white high-top sneakers and wool athletic socks.

"I've got the same sneakers upstairs," I told my father. "Eddie sells them in his store."

"Is that a fact?" he asked, pleased to be in style. "I'm told they're very popular this year. They make me jump a little higher. That's a very useful thing, I'm sure."

To demonstrate his point, my father jumped a foot or so off the ground and tried to touch the ceiling. He missed by several inches and twisted his ankle on the way down.

Just this brief exercise made my father break out in sweat. My father had always preferred cold weather when he was alive. In the summertime, when other families spent their vacations at the beach, we traveled north, where the mountain peaks were covered with freshly fallen snow and the air was cool all year round.

We went to sit in the living room, my father settling into his favorite green leather chair, me right beside him on the bench to our old piano. We talked for several minutes about nothing in particular, without settling on any single topic. It was the first time since my father's death that we'd had any difficulty making conversation.

"Eddie has a swell house," my father remarked.

"Not too bad, I guess," I replied. "Nothing special."

"He's a nice man," my father said. "Eddie, I mean."

"I suppose," I said, without much enthusiasm.

"You like him, don't you?" my father asked. "You like him very much?"

"I wasn't expecting you," I answered, trying to change the subject.

"Well, I've never given you much in the way of notice," he replied.

"I wish I knew when you were coming sometimes," I complained. "You know, so I could be a little more prepared."

"You must have some idea how it works by now, David," my father said. "I generally make an appearance whenever you've got a problem so big it takes both of us to solve it."

"You're *supposed* to be here all the time," I complained, "not just when I need you."

"Yes, that would be best," my father agreed. "But that's not exactly what's troubling you this time."

I detected a strange tone in my father's voice, as though he already knew things that hadn't yet occurred to me.

"You've got a different sort of difficulty this time, David," he continued. "A very sensitive matter we ought to get right out in the open."

"I don't know what you're talking about," I said, not quite sure if I was telling him the truth.

"Come on, now," my father urged me. "We've always been honest with each other."

"Samuel's the problem," I blurted out, anxious to stop my father from going any further. "I'm sure you'll just tell me to make the best of it. Like you did with Eddie."

"I was right about Eddie, wasn't I?" he asked.

I shrugged my shoulders, refusing to admit to anything. But it was true, I had adjusted very well to Eddie, much better than I had expected.

"Samuel's the problem," I repeated more forcefully.

"I don't think your little brother is really to blame," my father said. "Someday, though I know it's hard to imagine when, I'm guessing you might even start to like Samuel just a little."

"Well, you can obviously read my mind," I said sarcastically. "So what's wrong with me?"

"You've run into an unexpected problem you're not quite sure how to handle," my father explained. "This particular problem concerns both Eddie Kravitz and me."

"You and Eddie?" I asked. "You don't even know each other."

"Don't feel guilty," my father said. "This sort of thing happens all the time."

"Guilty?" I said angrily. "Why should I feel guilty?"

"You shouldn't," my father said.

"I don't," I insisted.

My father lifted himself out of the chair and sat next to me on the bench. Instead of continuing the conversation, he played the piano. His short, fat fingers danced gracefully along the keyboard, which was really amazing, since my father had never learned to play the piano when he was alive. I recognized the music immediately. My father was playing Eddie's favorite songs, show tunes mostly, with an occasional lullaby mixed in-between.

"You've become awfully fond of Eddie and that worries you," my father explained. "Samuel has a father and you don't. Sometimes you think it might be nice if Eddie were your father. You might even occasionally wish you didn't belong to me at all."

"It's not true," I said. "None of it."

"You don't miss me quite like you used to, and that's a little frightening," my father said.

"You're wrong," I insisted. "You don't know everything. How do you know these things?"

My father stopped playing. "Because you want

me to know," he answered, wrapping his flabby arms around my shoulders. "And that's what matters most, David."

I wanted to tell him that he was wrong, that Eddie Kravitz meant nothing to me. It wasn't as though I had stopped loving my father, but he had been dead and gone for more than five years. I still missed him, maybe not every day, not as often as before, or as much as I should, but I could change all that, I knew I could. If I concentrated just a little bit harder, I could miss my father more than ever—every hour of the day, every minute in fact, just like he deserved.

Besides, Eddie Kravitz wasn't so great. He knew nothing about painting or art, and he couldn't shoot a basketball to save his life. Once Samuel was old enough to go camping, or to learn to dance the polka, Eddie wouldn't have any more use for me. I was David Connors, Steven Connors's son. My father wasn't supposed to be forgotten for one single second just because he was gone.

"I'm sorry," I told my father. It wasn't much of an explanation, but under the circumstances, it was the best that I could do.

"Don't be," my father said. "I'm really very pleased."

"It hurts to think of you sometimes," I explained.

"I know it does," he said. "Someday, perhaps, it won't be quite so painful for you."

"I wish I could see you more often," I told him. "Then I'm sure I'd miss you all the time."

"I wish you could, too," my father agreed. "But you need your family and they need you."

"Eddie's not my father," I reminded him.

"No, he's not," my father agreed. "But he's part of your family and he's awfully fond of you."

When I didn't respond, my father said, "Tell me about him. Tell me about Eddie."

I thought about describing Eddie as only average, or maybe even below, but I knew the better I made him sound, the more pleased my father would be.

"Well, he doesn't order me around," I told my

father. “I get to decide how much TV to watch, when to do my homework and go to bed, and whether I want to cut my hair. We take care of Samuel and help each other do things, grown-up things mostly. He treats me like a . . . a . . .”

“Friend?” my father said.

“Friend?” I said back, considering my father’s answer. “I guess you could say that.”

“It sounds to me like there might be one or two advantages to growing up,” my father remarked.

“Maybe a few,” I replied.

“Now, you don’t really believe Eddie’s going to stop being your friend all of a sudden?” my father asked. “That doesn’t sound like any friend I know.”

“I hope not,” I answered him.

“So you’ve got Eddie for a friend, and you’ve got Mr. Paul for a friend, and you’ve got your mother, and you’ve got a little brother, who believe it or not, makes a lot less noise than a certain little boy I remember. All in all, that’s not too terribly bad, is it?”

“Not too terribly bad,” I confessed.

"And you can have me all for yourself, if you still want me."

"I do want you," I told my father, and suddenly, I wanted him more than ever. "Will you stop coming now? Because of what I said?"

"You can't get rid of me that easily," he replied. "I'm still your father, aren't I?"

"Yes," I answered.

"I'm happy to hear you say that, David," my father said. "Because I'd like you to get a haircut. Tomorrow. Nice and short."

"Yes, sir," I replied obediently, not once mentioning to my father that he should do the same.

"And I don't want you watching television before you've finished your homework. Understood?"

"You're being unreasonable," I complained.

"Maybe so," he nodded happily. "But that's a father's job."

After my father finished his lunch, we played a game of chess. I had him cornered and was just about to steal his queen when my brother woke up from his nap with the usual hysterical scream. My father helped me feed Samuel and change his diaper. We made funny faces and sang songs about dragons and pirates and mermaids, but Samuel still wouldn't quiet down.

"When you were Samuel's age, I used to read to you," my father said. "Worked every time."

"It's worth a try," I agreed. "Pick something from the bookcase."

My father handed me *The Night Before Christmas*.

"Not that," I complained. "Are you crazy?"

"Why not?" he asked innocently. "It used to be your favorite."

"It's not my favorite now," I said. "Besides, it's February. Christmas is ten months away."

"That's ridiculous," my father said, laughing. "Samuel thinks it's Christmas all year round."

"It's the day you died," I whispered to my father.

"You can't blame that on Christmas, David," he replied loudly. "I'm sure there's no connection at all."

"You read it if you want to hear it so much," I told him. "I refuse."

"Don't mind if I do," he said.

My father struggled to fit his oversized body into the small chair next to Samuel's crib. Just as my father started to read, I interrupted him.

"Aren't you forgetting that you're invisible to everybody else?" I asked my father. "Samuel won't be able to hear you."

"Now that's the strangest thing," he replied. "It turns out that small children can see and hear me, too. Did I neglect to mention that?"

"Yes, you did," I said. My father was smiling from ear to ear. "You neglect to mention lots of things." But for the first time in months, I was smiling, too.

In a deep, soft, slow voice, my father began to read. I used one of Samuel's stuffed bears as a pillow and lay face down on the floor, pretending not to listen. By the time my father had reached the part about the children nestled all snug in their beds, Samuel was asleep. I drifted off after the arrival of the little old driver with his miniature sleigh and eight tiny reindeer. When I woke up a few hours later, my father was gone.

That night at dinner, Eddie asked me to help him build a patio in the backyard. I told him I could start the next day, right after I got my hair cut. Nice and short.

Chapter Five

Mr. Paul was sick for a full year before he died, at the age of eighty-two. It happened just ten days before the start of winter, and I was twelve years old.

His death didn't come as a surprise to anyone. It happened slowly, just the way the doctors had predicted. In the beginning, as long as he took his medicine, Mr. Paul could work at his desk for hours and take his usual two-mile walk around the neighborhood. But after a few months he grew weaker and walked only half as far. Then, he stopped walking altogether and took long afternoon naps, sometimes sleeping until supper. A little while later, Mr. Paul lost the strength to punch a typewriter or to drag his pen across the page. He talked into a tape recorder and a secretary came in twice a week to type his tired words. By the end, his voice was a whisper and it hurt him just to open his eyes.

We had moved to the country, and it took me two and a half hours to reach Mr. Paul's house by bike. I went every Saturday morning, arriving no later than nine, and stayed until Sunday, leaving after the supper dishes were cleaned and put away.

We didn't waste the precious time we had together. In the mornings I painted while Mr. Paul wrote his book. I watched Mr. Paul closely while he worked, carefully noting every detail of his appearance and each little movement and gesture he made. I studied his peculiar egg-shaped head and the texture and feel of his white, wrinkled skin. When Mr. Paul laughed, I noticed that his loose, enormous ears flapped up and down like a sea gull's wings preparing for takeoff. Every hour or so, he would rub his bald scalp with the palm of one hand, as though testing to see if he'd grown any hair. If he was napping during the day, Mr. Paul slept with the left eye open and the right eye closed, but at nighttime it was the other way around.

With a brush as my camera, I painted at least a hundred different pictures of Mr. Paul. Just in case Mr. Paul wasn't permitted to visit me after his death, I was determined to remember him forever.

Mr. Paul's nurse took the weekends off, and I cooked all our meals. Every Thursday night I telephoned Mr. Paul, and he would place his orders. I made us spaghetti with homemade tomato sauce, chicken teriyaki, corned beef and cabbage, and tuna fish surprise. My recipe for swiss cheese meat loaf was Mr. Paul's favorite. And I always made sure we had a large pitcher of iced tea with extra lemon, which we would drink all day long.

I gave Mr. Paul his medicine four times a day: two small yellow pills and one large pink pill shaped like a shrunken hot dog. Every two hours, I took his temperature. If Mr. Paul felt a sharp pain in his chest, I would hold his hand and whistle something silly or soothing until it passed. I was a lousy whistler, and after a few months, Mr. Paul asked me if I would mind reciting poetry instead. When Mr. Paul had trouble walking, I would carry him to his bedroom in an old red wheelbarrow. I checked in on Mr. Paul at least two times a night, just to be sure that he was still there.

I liked taking care of Mr. Paul. Watching him die wasn't easy or fun, but when the time came, I was glad that his death hadn't been a surprise. I felt important, even lucky, knowing that Mr. Paul had depended on me at the end of his life, as I had depended on him at the beginning of mine. For the past six years, Mr. Paul had been my father, grandfather, teacher, and friend all rolled into one, and I was grateful for the chance to give back even a small portion of all the kindness I had received. I was starting to realize that giving could be just as good as getting when the people I loved were involved, and with Mr. Paul, giving and getting were one and the same.

Mr. Paul was racing to complete his biography of Theodore Roosevelt, the twenty-sixth president of the United States. It was his last and most important book, he said, and he stubbornly refused to die before it was finished.

"It's a personal matter between T. R. and me," he explained.

Mr. Paul had been a sickly child. He'd had polio, tuberculosis, and fevers so strange and hot that he'd lost all his hair. When he was six, Mr. Paul caught pneumonia, and the doctors told his family that he would never recover.

Mr. Paul met Theodore Roosevelt on Christmas morning in the year 1900, when Roosevelt was the governor of New York. He arrived just after dawn at the hospital in Brooklyn where Mr. Paul was a patient. The children had prepared cardboard Christmas cards for the governor, but Mr. Paul was too weak to finish his, and he buried the card beneath his pillow, where no one would find it. But when Teddy Roosevelt caught sight of the bald, pasty-faced little boy who was struggling to breathe, he headed straight for Mr. Paul's bed and sat down beside him.

"What are you in for, little one?" Teddy Roosevelt asked.

"You name it, I've had it," Mr. Paul replied faintly. "This time it's pneumonia, I think."

"Bully for you," he said. "Can't let a little thing like pneumonia keep you down." And for the next few minutes, Theodore Roosevelt spoke privately with the six-year-old Mr. Paul.

"You know, I'm no stranger to sickness myself," Teddy Roosevelt said. "When I was a boy your age, I had asthma so bad I couldn't get out of bed. People used to say I'd never lead a normal life. . . . Well, they were absolutely right. There's been absolutely, positively nothing *normal* about it."

Teddy Roosevelt laughed so hard at this remark that the nurses had to ask him to please quiet down.

"What happened?" Mr. Paul whispered anxiously. "How did you get well?"

"I made up my mind to do it, pure and simple,"

Teddy Roosevelt boasted. "The mind is the key. Just close your eyes and imagine yourself feeling better already. You can make almost anything happen."

"They say I'm too sick," Mr. Paul explained.

"Balderdash!" Teddy Roosevelt exclaimed. "You've got your whole life ahead of you, son."

"I'm not so sure," Mr. Paul said suspiciously.

"What would you like to be when you're all grown-up?"

"I don't know," Mr. Paul responded, still not convinced that he needed to give the matter much thought. "I do like to read."

"A writer, I think," Teddy Roosevelt declared after a moment of careful consideration. "That's the ticket for this particular young man."

"And what would you like to be, sir, when you're all grown-up?" Mr. Paul asked Teddy Roosevelt.

For a rare moment, never to be repeated again, Teddy Roosevelt was speechless. Looking absolutely puzzled and perplexed, he stretched and pulled at his thick, bushy mustache, pondering Mr. Paul's question.

"I don't . . . I mean, I haven't given the matter much thought," Teddy Roosevelt stammered timidly. "I do like to talk."

"You'll be president of the United States someday," Mr. Paul decided. "That's the ticket for you."

"President," Teddy Roosevelt repeated, practicing the sound of that wonderful word. Roosevelt's eyes danced with excitement as he thought about the notion.

"And why not?" he concluded. "If I put my mind to it."

"The mind is the key," Mr. Paul agreed.

"Have we got ourselves a deal then?" Teddy Roosevelt asked. "One president, one writer, and no more loafing around for either one of us. The next time I come to visit, I don't expect to see the likes of you."

"It's a deal," Mr. Paul said.

Mr. Paul reached under his pillow and pulled out the unfinished Christmas card.

"Merry Christmas," he said as he handed the card to Teddy Roosevelt.

In red crayon, Mr. Paul had started to draw a picture of Santa Claus preparing for his annual ride. But the reindeer were missing, as well as the sack of presents, and he hadn't been able to find a white crayon for Santa Claus's beard.

"It's not very good," Mr. Paul said apologetically. "I promise I'll be a much better writer."

"Most unusual, most unusual," Teddy Roosevelt remarked as he carefully studied the card. "This fat fellow you've drawn here, he looks a little like me."

Teddy Roosevelt wrote a one-line note across Santa's stomach and returned the card to Mr. Paul.

"You take it," Teddy Roosevelt said. "For good luck. Who knows? Someday maybe you'll write a book about me."

Teddy Roosevelt grabbed Mr. Paul's weak, bony hand and shook it firmly, as though the boy was already completely well.

"Thank you for coming," Mr. Paul said.

"Dee-lighted," was Teddy Roosevelt's one-word reply.

❄ ❄ ❄ ❄

Good luck came quickly to both of them. A year after their brief visit, Teddy Roosevelt was president of the United States, and Mr. Paul was well. Though I must admit I never quite saw the resemblance, Teddy Roosevelt always looked exactly like Santa Claus to Mr. Paul.

"Why did you wait so long to write the book?" I asked Mr. Paul when he had finished his story.

"It's taken me all these years to understand Teddy Roosevelt's life," he answered me. "I didn't want to begin until I could see the complete picture."

"If you could make yourself feel better then, why can't you do it now?" I asked Mr. Paul.

"It wasn't my turn to die when I was a boy," Mr. Paul explained. "But now, my time has come. I'm ready and willing."

"What about my father?" I asked. "Why couldn't he decide to make himself well?"

"We don't always have a choice about the things that happen to us, no matter how hard we try," Mr. Paul replied.

"I know my father was sorry about dying," I said, without revealing how I had learned this important bit of information.

"Maybe the people who leave here too early finish out their lives somewhere else," Mr. Paul suggested. "I believe some of us have the opportunity to achieve great things after our deaths."

"I don't know what my father does exactly," I said to Mr. Paul. "He hasn't ever told me."

"Perhaps you should ask him when you get the chance," Mr. Paul responded, as though this idea wasn't the least bit unusual.

"What will you do once you're dead?" I asked Mr. Paul.

"I think I'd like to rest, David," he replied. "I've lived a long time. It's given me the privilege to know fascinating people like yourself and Mr. Theodore Roosevelt all in one lifetime. And once I finish this book, I will have completed the last of my Mount Rushmore biographies."

"Mount Rushmore?" I asked him. "You mean the place with the presidents?"

"Carved in stone in the Black Hills of South Dakota are the heads of four of our greatest presidents," Mr. Paul explained. "When my present task is complete, I will have written a book about the distinguished lives of each one of those great men. It's my proudest achievement."

"It must be a beautiful mountain," I said.

"So I'm told," Mr. Paul replied sadly. "I've never actually seen it."

"You haven't?" I asked. "Why not?"

"I planned on visiting Mount Rushmore many times, but unfortunately, one thing or another always got in the way. I'm afraid it's too late now."

"Perhaps you can visit the mountain after you die," I suggested.

"That, David, is a splendid idea," Mr. Paul said, his bright pink eyes burning with anticipation. "I can catch up on my rest a little while later."

Three weeks after this conversation, Mr. Paul and I celebrated Christmas. We didn't actually call it Christmas, and in fact, we held it on the first of December. I still hated December the twenty-fifth, and Mr. Paul didn't think he would last another twenty-four days.

We placed our presents underneath a cactus plant in Mr. Paul's study. My gift to Mr. Paul was large and light and shaped like a poster. His gift to me was small and square and even lighter. First, we ate dinner. I roasted the smallest duck I could find and served it with mashed potatoes, smothered in butter and brown gravy. For dessert, we had plum pudding. Mr. Paul could barely eat, but he asked me to load his plate with enough food to feed three large, healthy people, just so I would know how much he appreciated my effort.

With my help, Mr. Paul opened his present first. Inside the cardboard cylinder was a painting of Mount Rushmore big enough to cover one of Mr. Paul's bedroom walls. I had used a picture in an old geography book as a model. Lincoln's long, crooked nose and craggy cheeks were tough to copy, but Jefferson and Washington hadn't given me too much trouble. I spent most of my time on Theodore Roosevelt's strong, smiling, spectacled face, and even though the likeness wasn't perfect, it was *my* proudest achievement.

"David, from this day forward, this painting shall be my most prized possession," Mr. Paul said softly. "With your paintbrush, you've taken me to the top of that wonderful mountain."

When I opened the small square box, I discovered that I was now the proud owner of Mr. Paul's most prized possession since 1900, the Christmas card autographed by Theodore Roosevelt.

The thin cardboard paper was yellow and torn, and I had trouble making out the words. I removed the plastic covering and studied the inscription.

To Henry Paul:
Good luck. Good health. Bully.
T. R.

Until that moment I had never known Mr. Paul's first name. For the next ten days of his life, he asked me to call him Henry.

On December ninth, Henry Paul the writer

completed the biography of Theodore Roosevelt. He died two days later, staring at my painting of Mount Rushmore on his bedroom wall. As his time drew nearer, I asked Mr. Paul if he was frightened.

"No, David, not at all," he replied in a soft, peaceful voice. "When I close my eyes, I can imagine myself feeling better already."

At the end, I took Mr. Paul's weak, bony hand in mine and held it firmly, as though he was already completely well.

"Have a nice death, Henry," I said to Mr. Paul. "Thank you for living."

"Dee-lighted," was Mr. Paul's one-word reply.

And in an instant, he was gone.

More than five hundred people attended Mr. Paul's funeral. Some were famous celebrities and politicians I had read about in the newspapers. Most were just ordinary neighbors and friends. But everyone in attendance had been touched by the distinguished life of the biographer Henry Paul.

At the cemetery, after everyone else had gone

back to their cars, I threw a single red rose on Mr. Paul's grave. Just as I was ready to leave, a second rose flew over my head and landed next to mine. I knew without even looking that my father had arrived.

"Sorry I couldn't get here sooner, David," my father said to me. "It's a busy time of year."

"I'm going to miss him," I said, holding back my tears.

"I'll always be grateful to him for looking after you," my father said.

"I knew he was going to die," I said. "But I guess I never stopped hoping he would live forever."

"And he will, David," my father promised cheerfully. "But Mr. Paul's time here was over. You understand that now, don't you?"

"Yes, I think I do," I said. "I'm happy for him. But I know he won't be coming back to visit me."

"You two are the best of friends already," my father said. "You can talk with Mr. Paul whenever you like. He's listening to every word you have to say."

My father held me gently in his arms. His sharp beard scratched my cheeks, but I didn't mind a bit.

My father's stomach was a little larger now, and I had to hug him extra tight just to reach around his waist.

My father and I held hands and walked across the cemetery until we unexpectedly came to his grave. The bottom of the granite stone was covered with dirt and dead weeds. I hadn't been to visit my father's grave for the entire time that Mr. Paul was sick, and I quickly knelt down and began pulling out the weeds.

"Who planted these?" my father asked. He was pointing to two miniature evergreen trees on each side of the headstone. "They look like tiny Christmas trees."

"It might have been me," I confessed reluctantly. "And they are *not* Christmas trees."

My father spoke in a gentle whisper, but his voice was deep and sure. "You're growing up very nicely, David," he said. "In case I hadn't mentioned that before."

I continued pulling out the weeds around my father's grave but he reached out his hand to stop me. "It's not necessary, David," he said. "I'm perfectly comfortable."

We lay down together on the cold ground, resting our heads against the stone and staring up at the cold winter sky.

I felt confused about how life treats different people differently. "You didn't live to be old," I said to my father. "Not even half as old as Mr. Paul."

"Ah, but look at what I accomplished," my father said, beaming proudly at me.

"I wish I could have done something kind for you when you were here," I told my father.

"You've been taking very good care of me since my death," my father replied.

"I never gave you anything," I said.

"David, every time I see you taking care of the people you love, it's as though you're doing it for me," my father replied.

I reached inside my coat pocket and took out the Christmas card autographed by Theodore Roosevelt.

"Take this," I said, handing the card to my father.

He examined the picture of Santa Claus carefully and read the inscription.

"No, David," he said. "This is Mr. Paul's card. He wanted you to have it. You keep it. For good luck."

"Are you sure?" I asked. "I want you to have something that belongs to me."

"I already do," he said, not explaining what he meant. He handed back Mr. Paul's card. "Who knows? Someday maybe you'll make a Christmas card for me."

My father stood up and started leaping over the tops of the headstones in his row like a ballet dancer—the fattest ballet dancer in history. I called out a good-bye before my father was out of sight.

"No need for that, David," he called back, waving his hands wildly while trying to balance his body on a very narrow stone. "We'll be seeing each other again."

I stayed at the cemetery until dark, resting my head on my father's grave and chatting with Mr. Paul.

Chapter Six

It was Christmas Eve, and I hadn't seen my father in four years. After so much time, I had given up hope that we would ever meet again. My brother Samuel was six years old now, the same age I had been when Christmas died for me. But for two weeks running, I had been the one who had been acting like the child.

After Samuel was born, I persuaded my mother and Eddie to keep treating Christmas like it was just another ordinary holiday, not as special as Thanksgiving or a birthday, and only slightly more important than Groundhog Day. Fortunately for me, Samuel had been too young to complain.

But this year was different. From everything he had heard at school or had seen on TV, Samuel had suddenly gotten the idea that Christmas was supposed to be the most wonderful day of the year, and he insisted that his family start treating the holiday with all the attention it deserved. I did my best to squelch my brother's rebellion, but on every family vote we took, I lost by a landslide.

First Samuel convinced Eddie to crawl on his belly across our snow-covered roof to hang row after row of blinking red and green lights so that Santa Claus and his silly reindeer wouldn't miss us in the dark.

Then Samuel made our mother decorate the house like an old-fashioned picture he had seen on a Christmas card. Hanging above the fireplace in the living room was an enormous green wreath, and smaller wreaths hung from every door. Thick branches of fresh evergreen were wrapped around the railing leading up the stairs, and blooming red-and-white poinsettias sat on every end table. The front door was wrapped in "Merry Christmas" paper and tied with a red satin bow, like an oversized present. Outside on the lawn was a giant sled filled with fake presents, with a six-foot tall, pipe-smoking Santa dressed in red suspenders and blue jeans standing next to his vehicle.

My pesky brother even persuaded *me* to go into town with him so that he could present the phony Santa Claus with his list of extravagant demands. Since I had no intention of getting or giving gifts that year, I didn't listen to Samuel as he rattled off his requests. But when Samuel was through, I couldn't help noticing how the phony Santa Claus patted him on the head and handed him a candy cane, without making any promises.

"I know he's just an assistant to the *real* Santa Claus," Samuel said to me as we walked away, and two twin girls took Samuel's place on the so-called Santa's lap. "But do you think he'll give Santa the message?"

"I wouldn't be surprised," I told my brother, knowing full well that Eddie and my mother would see to it that Samuel wasn't disappointed.

"He wasn't even taking notes," Samuel said, understandably puzzled.

"He must have a really good memory," I replied, unable to think up a better explanation.

But when Samuel advised my mother and Eddie that a two-foot tall tree on the table in the hallway was not what he'd had in mind, someone had to draw the line. First, I suggested that we buy an artificial tree. If the tree wasn't living, I explained to my brother, there would never be any mess or unwelcome surprises, and year after year it would always be the perfect size and shape. But Samuel insisted that we get a real tree. Before I knew what had happened, the four of us were heading north in Eddie's crowded convertible, and I was being tortured by a six-year-old and a shoe salesman singing carols in my ear.

We drove to a farm where Christmas trees were raised just like vegetables and flowers. I stubbornly sat in the car while Eddie, my mother, and Samuel spent a full hour walking around outside in the cold, looking for just the right tree. Using a rusty, toothless saw, Eddie cut down the tallest tree in sight, a blue spruce, and my mother and Samuel did their best to hold the beast's branches steadily in place. For another painful hour, Eddie, Samuel, and my mother struggled to tie down the huge tree to the flimsy top of Eddie's little car. We drove home slowly in the snowy, icy dark—stopping, as usual, for every yellow light.

It was still a full two weeks before Christmas, but Samuel insisted on trimming the tree at once. After the tree was screwed tightly in its stand, I got my revenge by pointing out each and every flaw.

"You didn't saw the trunk off evenly," I told Eddie. "It tilts to the right."

"Nonsense," my mother replied. "It's straight as an arrow. Besides, once all of the ornaments and tinsel are on, you won't notice a thing."

"I like it this way," Samuel said brightly. "We'll always know it's ours."

"It's scraping the ceiling," I said. "You'll have to cut off the branches on top and then it won't come to a point like it's supposed to."

"That's positively ridiculous," my mother protested. "We just have to cut off a few little pieces here and there, and once the star is on, no one will ever know the difference."

"And there's a hole right in the middle," I continued, determined to convince my family that the tree's condition was hopeless. "You forgot to make sure the tree was full from top to bottom and all the way around."

This time Eddie disagreed, but Samuel wasn't quite so sure.

"How could we have missed such a big hole?" Samuel asked, his voice cracking with disappointment.

"All we have to do is turn the bad side toward the wall," Eddie explained, twirling the tree exactly half a circle to illustrate his point. "And, *presto*, no more hole." Samuel was thrilled by this keen display of magic, and he laughed in delight.

"Just feel the needles," I said. "They're not moist. I'll bet by Christmas, half the tree will be gone and you'll cut your fingers on the branches."

"I'll give it water every day," Samuel promised, certain that the tree could be preserved with just a little extra care.

Eddie climbed the ladder and carelessly cut off the branches at the top of the tree. When he was through, Samuel handed him a long string of multicolored lights, and my mother replaced the broken bulbs.

My mother had brought down boxes of our old ornaments from the attic. Working slowly and carefully, my family removed ornaments from their newspaper wrappings and discussed where each would be hung. There were plastic partridges, little cardboard drummer boys, Styrofoam reindeer, and breakable china angels missing half a wing. Once all the ornaments were hung, and burned, brown popcorn strung along the branches, my family started in with the tinsel—one long, shiny, silver strand at a time until the tree was raining icicles.

Hours later, when everything was complete, Samuel offered me the honor of putting up the crystal star. Reluctantly, I tried to find a place for the star on top of the topless tree, but no matter what tricks I tried, the tiny star vanished into the darkness of the branches.

For the next two weeks, my family refused to give up on their tree. As promised, Samuel watered it regularly, sometimes twice a day. Eddie woke up extra early each morning and swept the floor so that Samuel wouldn't see the dozens of needles that had fallen through the night. Once, when my mother thought no one was watching, she moved the heaviest ornaments to the back of the tree, in the hope that the larger branches would drop down far enough to cover up the hole.

Finally it was Christmas Eve. My mother and Eddie told me that they understood if I wasn't ready to celebrate Christmas with Samuel's enthusiasm. But apparently Christmas was going to happen whether I played along or not. As my brother, stepfather, and mother laughed and teased one another while completing the evening's preparations, I concentrated on their lopsided, skimpy, dried-out tree, shivering timidly behind a solid wall of ice, all of my own making. For the first time in ten years, I began to wonder whether Christmas might be just a little bit more complicated than I had wanted to believe.

"I think I was wrong about the tree," I finally said to my family. "It's not too terrible."

"No, you were right all along, David," Samuel said sadly, taking all of us by surprise. "Half the needles must have fallen off by now."

"Not half, Samuel," I lied, suddenly regretting some of the cruel things I'd said. "Just a few."

"I can still see the hole in back," my brother added. "It didn't really disappear."

"Forget what I said before," I said to Samuel. But my apology came too late to make a difference.

"Next year, maybe we can buy that fake tree you wanted, David," Samuel said to me, and turned toward his parents. "That's my vote."

Now that he had faced the truth about the tree,

Samuel began to pepper Eddie and my mother with questions about Santa Claus. They were tough questions—questions I'd never thought to ask when I was six years old and my father was still alive.

"Daddy, what time at night does Santa Claus come?"

"Not until you're asleep," Eddie answered, careful not to be too specific.

"Does David have to be asleep, too?" Samuel asked.

"Yep," Eddie replied. "David, too."

"Has Santa already been to other people's houses?" Samuel asked.

"Yes," my mother said, taking over for Eddie when he took too long to answer. "He's busy all night long."

"Then how do you know when he'll get here?" Samuel wanted to know. "And how will he know when we're asleep?"

"He'll just know, buddy," Eddie said, worn out by Samuel's persistence. "He'll just know."

"Santa Claus never arrives in this area until after

midnight," my mother added, trying to improve on Eddie's response. "If you're covering the whole world, you've got to follow an awfully tight schedule."

But my brother wasn't satisfied. "If Santa Claus is out there delivering presents before it's even bedtime, how come *those* kids don't have to be asleep?"

"When it's daytime here, it's the middle of the night somewhere else in the world," Eddie responded, proud to have thought so quick on his feet.

"What if we're not asleep when he comes?" Samuel asked.

"He only stops if you're sleeping," my mother replied, repeating what Eddie had said before.

"But suppose it's not my fault, like I had to go to the bathroom?" Samuel asked. "What happens then—no Christmas?"

My mother and Eddie had fallen right into the trap Samuel had set for them. I was proud of my brother for being such a smart and curious kid, but I also felt like a heel, knowing that Samuel wouldn't be so worried now if it hadn't been for me.

"He'll find a way to get here," I said to Samuel, smiling at my mother and Eddie. "No matter what you do."

After Samuel put on his pajamas and was ready for bed on a six-year-old kid's worst sleeping night of the year, he asked one final question.

"Is there *really* a Santa Claus?"

Samuel's voice was filled with doubt, and just a little trace of hope.

"Of course there's—" Eddie started to say, but Samuel interrupted him.

"No. I want David to tell me," he said, sitting up bravely in his bed. "Come on, David, I can take it."

From the time Samuel had been old enough to speak, my mother and Eddie had told him the usual lies about Santa Claus, and he had believed their every word. Instead of telling Samuel that Santa Claus was a fraud, I had kept quiet, and luckily for me, my brother had never bothered to ask me for my opinion. But now, Samuel only trusted his older brother to answer his question honestly, probably because I hadn't hesitated to tell him the ugly truth about his ugly tree.

Looking at my little brother, trying so hard to be brave, it suddenly occurred to me that I had been trying bit by bit to destroy Christmas for him, so that his fantasies wouldn't last one minute longer than mine had. At Samuel's age, I had lost Santa Claus and my father all in one night. But Samuel still had both, and I was jealous of his joy. Samuel could believe in fairy tales for just as long as he wanted, and when he eventually found out that Santa Claus was his father, he probably wouldn't mind at all.

To be sure that Samuel would get to stay a kid just as long as he pleased, I decided to tell my brother a lie, wishing more than ever that it could have been the truth. "Of course there's a Santa Claus," I said. "What a dopey question. Who else would bring the two of us so many presents?"

"Are you sure?" Samuel asked, still not quite convinced.

"Surer than sure," I promised.

"It doesn't make much sense, David," Samuel

observed, worried that I had joined ranks with Eddie and my mother, who did not always behave sensibly.

"That's true," I agreed. "But sometimes, the most incredible things happen, and they're no less real."

"I don't know," Samuel said suspiciously.

I boasted to my brother about the vast experience I'd gained in my sixteen years on earth. "When you get to be my age," I said, "you'll see for yourself."

Convinced that older kids were just about the smartest people on the planet, Samuel finally took my word for it on the subject of Santa Claus.

I watched as Eddie and my mother tucked Samuel into bed and kissed him good night, warning him for at least the hundredth time not to open any presents without waking them first.

When Samuel's door was closed and we were together downstairs, Eddie, my mother, and I got to work wrapping Samuel's presents for the morning. Santa Claus was about to bring my brother a bookcase filled with children's biographies about the presidents, a ten-record set of "Great Broadway

Show Tunes," a miniature pool table, a catcher's mitt, a hockey stick, and a new camera.

When I joked that my little brother's Christmas list was perhaps a little extravagant, my mother handed me a crumpled sheet of red construction paper. She said it was the Christmas list that Samuel had read to the phony Santa on our trip into town. She had found the paper hidden under Samuel's mattress, where he thought no one would find it. To my surprise, his list contained only one request, written in green crayon: *Please let my brother David like X-mas this year.*

I read my brother's Christmas wish a dozen times before I excused myself and headed off to bed. I reminded my mother and Eddie that *both* Samuel and I had to be asleep before Santa Claus could come.

Sometime in the middle of the night I heard a loud crash downstairs. I sprang from my bed to see what was the matter, and when I got to the top of the stairs, I saw my father.

He was sprawled out in the hallway, looking disheveled and a little dazed. My father was dressed in a black overcoat and gray wool pants, which he had tucked inside a pair of black rubber galoshes. On his head, he wore a red-checkered cap with silly-looking flaps drooping down well below his ears.

"It's snowing like crazy outside, David," he said happily. "Looks like we're going to have a white Christmas this year."

"Where have you been?" I asked as I made my way downstairs.

"Busy, dreadfully busy," he replied. "It's not easy getting around in all this weather."

"I don't mean tonight," I said. "Where have you been for the past four years?"

"Here and there," my father responded thoughtfully, scratching his very full beard. "Mostly there, I guess. When you're not alive, it gets a little tricky accounting for the time."

"I thought you were never coming back."

"Did you?" my father asked, with a note of surprise. "I told you we'd see each other again."

"You neglected to mention it would take so long," I said sarcastically.

"That's how long you needed," my father said. "It's perfectly fine. No need to apologize. Fortunately for the two of us, I wasn't pressed for time."

I started to ask my father why on earth I should be apologizing because *he* hadn't found time to visit me, but he interrupted me before I could get the words out.

"Aren't you even going to invite me to sit down, David?" he asked. "My goodness, your manners could certainly stand a little improvement."

"Go ahead," I replied. "Sit down. Make yourself comfortable."

My father got to work at the fireplace, and in what seemed only a minute, he was rubbing his hands fast and furiously in front of the fire, his teeth chattering from the cold. By the time he removed his hat and coat and the wet boots from his feet, his entire body was shaking, as though he had been wandering outside in the snow for hours. I offered him a heavy wool blanket, which he gladly accepted, and a cup of eggnog, but he preferred something hot instead.

My father looked older, four years' worth to be exact. His hair had turned almost completely gray, and his movements were slower and more precise. His long messy beard still covered most of his face, but the soft pink skin underneath had become more wrinkled and rough. His voice was softer now, though still plenty deep, and he had gained another ten or twelve pounds. He waddled slightly from side to side when he walked, like an oversized penguin with too much weight in the center and not much of anything else up top or down below.

His eyes were the same, though, just as I remembered them—a brilliant blue, like the calmest of seas. And they twinkled like two distant stars forever steering his way.

"Have you been content since we last met, David?" my father asked, once he was comfortable. "Everything up to snuff?"

"I guess so," I replied cautiously. "But you're only supposed to visit me if I'm unhappy or upset."

"So what's bothering you tonight?" he asked. "Why am I here now, do you think?"

I stopped to consider my father's question carefully. Earlier that night, I might have blamed Christmas for my problems, but I was actually looking forward to waking up and watching Samuel open gifts he hadn't even asked for.

"I'm not sure," I told my father, a little embarrassed by my confusion. "Don't get me wrong, I'm very glad to see you, but nothing, nothing at all, is bothering me."

And relieved to discover that it was absolutely true, I began to smile, then to laugh, harder and harder, louder and louder, until I nearly lost control. Never one to pass up an opportunity for amusement, my father quickly joined in, and soon, the two of us were absolutely giddy with delight.

Suddenly, though, I began to worry. In a moment, I stopped laughing. My father, on the other hand, was still enjoying our private little joke, and I had to shout to be heard above all his pleasure.

"So, why are you here?" I asked suspiciously.

"What's the trouble? There's something you haven't told me."

"Congratulations are in order," my father answered, still delirious with delight. "I've come to celebrate."

"I'm supposed to have a problem so big it takes both of us to solve it," I reminded my father. "Those are the rules. Remember?"

"The rules are whatever you want them to be, David," he said.

"You've never come to celebrate before," I said.

"You weren't ready," he replied. "You needed more time."

"Time for what?" I asked.

"Time to enjoy yourself a little," he explained. "Time to discover you don't really hate Christmas after all. Why, it's your favorite day of the year."

"I've hated Christmas since the day you died."

"So why have you stopped now?" he asked. "Christmas hasn't changed since I last checked, and as far as I know, I'm still dead."

"I've got to forget what happened to me," I said

seriously. "I can't go on ruining Christmas for everybody else."

"The way I ruined it for you?" my father asked.

"I didn't say that," I protested. But it was no use denying it; he knew what I meant.

"You haven't been angry with Christmas, David," my father said. "You've been angry with me."

It was true, every word he said. All this time, I had been blaming Christmas to avoid blaming him. I had never really forgiven my father for leaving me alone, as if he'd had any say in the matter.

"I'm not angry anymore," I told my father. "I'll always miss you, but I can't stay mad forever."

"David, I've been waiting an awfully long time to hear you say that," my father said.

"Is that why you came back to me?" I asked. "To change my feelings?"

"You did that all by yourself," my father explained. "You always had the power to bring me back, whenever you wanted. I didn't make the rules, David. You did."

Without another word, my father turned his

attention to our tree. Using his imagination—and just the right amount of magic—he fixed almost each and every flaw. At the top, he cut away more branches, except for one, until he shaped a new and better point. When I attached the crystal star, it shone brightly from above and cast a special glow on every branch below.

To cover up the hole in back, my father borrowed some branches from the railing leading up the stairs. With a hammer and some tacks, we attached the extra branches to the trunk until the tree looked full and thick from top to bottom and all the way around. As for the tree's dry condition, not even my father could bring back to life the dead needles that had already fallen to the ground. But he promised that the remaining needles would be fresh and healthy for as long as the tree was standing.

When I suggested using a saw to even out the stump, my father disagreed. Like Samuel, he preferred a tree that tipped, the more the better, and he gave me his solemn word that it would never fall.

As soon as the fire had dried his clothes, my father got dressed and started for the door.

"You're not using the window this time?" I asked.

"It's murder on my back," he said.

Before my father left, I knew we still had one last thing to talk about. When he fumbled for the words, I interrupted, knowing full well what he was trying to say.

"You won't be coming back again," I told him.

He bowed his head sadly but did not disagree.

"It's all right," I assured him. "I'm glad we got the extra time."

"Now that you and I know each other so well, David," my father said, "you'll find me everywhere you turn."

"Just use my imagination?" I asked.

"Exactly," my father said cheerfully. "That's the secret."

As we said our final good-bye, my father laughed out loud, a long, deep jolly laugh that would have woken my entire family if only they could have heard it.

"Merry Christmas, David," my father said. "I hope Santa brings you everything you want."

"He already has," I replied.

My father and I hugged tightly, and I kissed him on the lips. His beard was softer now and it tickled my cheeks.

"The two of us," I said to my father, stuttering out the words. "We did pretty well. Considering."

"Considering," my father said, "we did great."

"If I could only have one father," I told him, "I'm glad it was you."

"You'll always be my one and only son," my father said.

Lying awake in bed, I couldn't stop thinking about my father. I closed my eyes and tried to picture his gentle face, exactly as I had seen it only moments before. I wanted to be sure that I wouldn't forget a single detail of our last meeting together. I got up and turned on my lamp. I began to sketch first with a pencil, then with the paints, just as my father had taught me to do eight years ago. My memory was fresh, and my father's portrait took only a few minutes to complete.

As I stared at the rough painting, a strange thought occurred to me. I had seen this picture before, many times, but I couldn't say precisely where or when or how. When I sketched him again without the red-checkered cap, my father's hairy head looked a little more familiar. I noticed a strange resemblance to another man, an older gentleman whom I had never met before. I made my father's gray beard almost entirely white and added another ten or twelve pounds to his middle. Then I gave him a suit of red and white and something to get around in. And suddenly, I knew for sure.

Startled by my discovery, I ran from my bedroom and raced down the stairs. When I poked my head inside the living room, I could make out the shape of something large all alone beside the tree. It was resting against the fireplace for support, unable to stand on its own. I turned on the tree lights and saw the bicycle. Not just any bicycle, but a dark green Stingray with wide, thick wheels, a banana-shaped seat big enough for two, and three different gears for pedaling up and down hills. It wasn't scratched or bent, and I could see my face in the handlebars, they were so shiny and new.

My father must have dug out the Stingray from its snowy grave and taken it with him, wherever he had gone. He had fixed the damage I had done and polished the steel until the bike was even brighter and better than new. And now that I finally knew how to enjoy my gift from long ago, my father had returned it just in time for Christmas morning. Once I screwed on the kickstand I had kept under my bed for the past ten years, the bicycle was complete.

As I jumped on the bike and started to ride around the living room, I heard the guilty giggle of a six-year-old boy. I rode into the hallway and turned on the light, just as Samuel was tiptoeing down the stairs.

"Didn't Mom and Eddie tell you not to open any presents without waking them first?" I asked him.

"Has he been here, David?" Samuel asked anxiously. "Did he really come?"

I didn't have the heart to keep Samuel in suspense a minute longer. "You be the judge of that," I said, and led the way into the living room.

Samuel nearly knocked me over trying to get to the doorway. But he stopped dead in his tracks and gazed in astonishment at his beloved tree. By the time Samuel could speak, Eddie and my mother had joined me at the bottom of the stairs.

"It's fixed!" Samuel exclaimed. "He fixed the tree! Look, look, Santa fixed the tree!" he said as he led our mother by the hand into the living room.

Eddie and my mother nodded in polite confusion, more stunned than anyone by the morning's developments.

"You couldn't have done it," Samuel said to Eddie. "Not in a million years."

Samuel was as sure as I was that Santa had been the one who brought new life to our once lifeless tree.

"Not in a million years," Eddie repeated in astonishment.

"He must be real," Samuel said.

"That's what we've been telling you all along," I said, claiming credit I didn't deserve.

"I can't see the hole in back," Samuel said. "It disappeared. And feel the needles, Daddy," Samuel urged Eddie, as he shook hands with the soft, healthy branches. "They're not even sharp. I bet they won't fall off ever again."

"I'll bet you're right," Eddie said.

"It's still our tree," Samuel continued. "You can tell from the tipping."

"I'm glad he didn't fix the tipping," my mother said.

"That would have been a terrible mistake," I agreed, smiling.

"It's a beautiful tree, Daddy," Samuel said.

"Better than I ever imagined," Eddie agreed, as a single tear of joy journeyed down his cheek.

"Don't be fooled by first appearances," I said to my brother, repeating a lesson it had taken me a very long time to learn. "Everything looks better once you see the complete picture."

After we were finished admiring the tree, Eddie and my mother directed Samuel to his presents.

"Whose bicycle is that?" Samuel asked.

"What a goofy question," I said to my brother. "You didn't really believe I wasn't getting you anything for Christmas, did you?"

"You mean it's mine?" Samuel asked in amazement.

"From you?" Eddie and my mother asked, every bit as amazed as Samuel.

"It's the funniest thing," I said to Samuel, remembering his wish. "Out of nowhere, I suddenly got the feeling that it might be fun to like Christmas this year."

"Now I know he's real," Samuel said, as happiness filled his freckled face.

I knew my mother recognized the bike, but she never said a word to me about it.

The sky outside was as blue as a gentle sea, and I watched the morning sun rise above the naked trees. Several inches of fresh snow had fallen during the night, making my ride on the bike a little slippery. I was six feet tall, and I had to bend my legs like a pretzel to pedal the tiny Stingray. The bike fit Samuel perfectly, and though it was my brother's first two-wheeler, he was riding circles around me by breakfast.

When Samuel and I returned from our ride, Eddie pulled me aside and asked how I had managed to fix the tree and buy an old bicycle, all in one night.

"It wasn't me," I told him.

"Well, who was it then?" he asked.

"Why, Santa Claus, of course," I replied. "I was just his helper."

I laughed out loud. It was a deep, throaty, jolly laugh, much deeper and jollier than I had ever laughed before.

Now that my unusual tale is finished, I don't know quite how to describe it. So let's just call it a Christmas card, written especially for my father. In my experience, Santa Claus can come in all shapes and sizes, depending on your need. To some, he might be tall and skinny and bald, nothing like his pictures. To others, he might be old like a grandfather or as young as a newborn infant. He could be a man or a woman, a relative or a stranger, even the twenty-sixth president of the United States. Why, he might not even be alive. But I believe in him, and you should, too. You go ahead and pick any person you want, but my father will always be Santa Claus to me.